A PILLOW
for
MY MOM

CHARISSA SGOUROS

A PILLOW *for* MY MOM

Illustrated by CHRISTINE ROSS

HOUGHTON MIFFLIN COMPANY BOSTON
1998

Walter Lorraine *wr* Books

Text copyright © 1998 by Charissa Sgouros
Illustrations copyright © 1998 by Christine Ross

Library of Congress Cataloging-in-Publication Data

Sgouros, Charissa.
  A pillow for my mom / by Charissa Sgouros; illustrated by
Christine Ross.
      p.   cm.
  Summary: A girl misses her mother, who is sick in the hospital.
  ISBN 0-395-82280-7
  [1. Sick — Fiction.   2. Mothers and daughters — Fiction.]   I. Ross,
Christine, ill.   II. Title.
PZ7.S5256Pi   1998   97-36077
[E] — dc21   CIP
                                                          AC

HOR   10 9 8 7 6 5 4 3 2 1
Printed in the United States of America

Dedicated to Joan P. Sgouros, the real writer in the family — C.S.

For Carla and Sam Gray in memory of Matthew — C.M.R.

My Mom got sick this summer.

She doesn't laugh the way she used to anymore.

I miss my Mom.

She used to read to me and play games with me.

She would tell me stories and I would tell her jokes.

She's in the hospital now.

When she sees me she smiles, but she tells
me that she's never really comfortable.

So I made her a special pillow.

I think it makes her feel more comfortable.

When she puts her head on it, she says
she thinks of me and smiles.

I have the pillow now.

I still miss my Mom,
but when I miss her the most . . .

I just put my head on the pillow and smile.